ROSAMUND

BY
Janice Johnson

ILLUSTRATIONS BY
Deborah Haeffele

SIMON & SCHUSTER BOOKS FOR YOUNG READERS
Published by Simon & Schuster
New York   London   Toronto   Sydney   Tokyo   Singapore

SIMON & SCHUSTER BOOKS FOR YOUNG READERS
1230 Avenue of the Americas, New York, New York 10020
Text copyright © 1994 by Janice Johnson.
Illustrations copyright © 1994 by Deborah Haeffele.
All rights reserved including the right of reproduction in whole
or in part in any form.
SIMON & SCHUSTER BOOKS FOR YOUNG READERS
is a trademark of Simon & Schuster. Designed by Paul Zakris
and Vicki Kalajian. The text for this book is set in 15-point
Cochin. The illustrations were done in oil paints.
Manufactured in the United States of America.
10 9 8 7 6 5 4 3 2 1

Library of Congress Cataloging-in-Publication Data
Johnson, Janice (Janice Kay)
    Rosamund / by Janice Johnson : illustrated by Deborah
Haeffele.
        p. cm.
    Summary: The seeds of a red and white English rose find their
way to Oregon to be planted by generations of Rosamunds.
    [1. Roses—Fiction.] I. Haeffele, Deborah, ill. II. Title
PZ7.J632164Ro 1994
[E]—dc20   92-44115 CIP AC
ISBN: 0-671-79329-2

For the roses in my
life, Sarah and Katie
                    —J.J.

To my family, Steve,
Christiane, and Cathryn,
and to Mary Bundy and the
Raleigh Little Theater
                    —D.H.

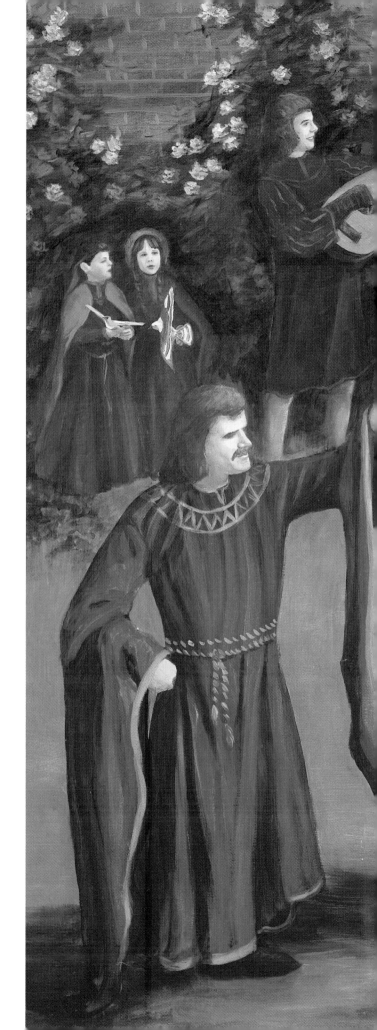

ong ago, when King Henry II ruled England, there came a glorious spring. Within the walls of a nobleman's sheltered garden, the buds swelled on the roses. But on one of the bushes, which grew just like the others, the buds appeared different.

ndeed, they were. Palest blush pink, swirled with crimson, the flowers were like nothing ever seen in England. Thus, the rose became known as Rosa Mundi, named for the nobleman's gentle wife, Rosamund. And from that time, daughters of the family were often named for their grandmothers, and for the rose.

One hundred years later it was a Lady Rosamund whose lord accepted the cross of the Crusader.

Bidding him farewell, she said, "I have embroidered the rose on your tunic and had it emblazoned upon your shield so that you will not forget your home, or me."

"I will not forget," he said, nor did he, and perhaps it was his longing for both that brought him safely home again.

In yet another century, England's peace was shattered when the War of the Roses was fought. On the one side was the white rose, on the other the red. Both rivals to England's throne called the lord of the manor to arms.

nder the summer sun he walked in the garden with his Lady Rosamund, trying to choose his way. He came to a bush whose branches were bowed beneath the weight of roses. The pink had faded to cream in the hot sun, while the crimson was still brilliant. He said, "Rosa Mundi holds both white and red."

"Perhaps," Lady Rosamund replied, "it is not meant that we should choose."

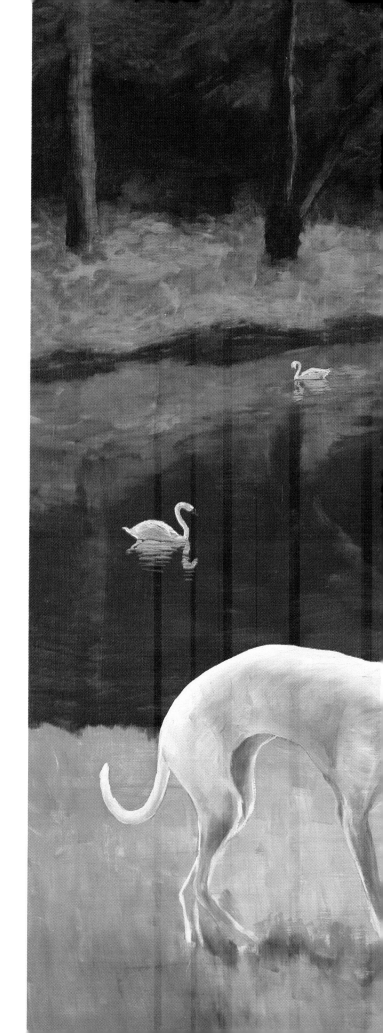

ndeed, as
though
guarded by
the rose, the
family did not fight. Yet
because they had stood
apart, they were no longer
favored. When hard years
came, the vast lands that
they had owned shrank.

he youngest child in the family was a girl named Rosamund, who loved the walled garden that now ran wild. But the time came when her father decided that the manor should be left to his younger brother and the family must board a ship bound for the New Land. As the day of departure neared, Rosamund's mother gathered seeds and slips from the garden to take with them. Rosamund herself took cuttings from her favorite rosebush.

o Rosa Mundi was left to tangle with the lavender and hollyhocks against the ancient stone walls of the manor. In a small plot carved from the wilderness that was now called Massachusetts, a cutting sent down roots into the rocky soil and grew fresh and strong.

This Rosamund's daughter bore only sons. By the time they had children of their own, her sons had forgotten their grandmother's name, though several took cuttings of the unusual striped rose when they hewed farms out of the New England forest.

In another one hundred and fifty years, the land was made up of small farms and villages and even cities that sent ships to round the globe. Each son had many sons and daughters, and there was not enough land for all to farm. Some became shipbuilders and merchants, but one dreamed of a new life in the Oregon Territory.

The way was dangerous, and his wife was able to take few possessions, but among them were seeds, and cuttings from her garden. Her baby was born during a night's stop out on the dusty prairie broken only by the muddy width of the Platte River. Holding the tiny newborn against her breast, the woman prayed for her daughter's life to be easier.

By the time Rose could walk, her parents had built a small log house on the banks of the broad Willamette River, surrounded by forest. At one corner of the vegetable garden grew hollyhocks and sunflowers and one spindly rose bush.

The log house grew as the forest fell, and finally it was replaced by a two-story white clapboard house that showed its age by the time Rose was an old lady. Beside the gate in the picket fence still grew the rose, though the vegetable garden was long gone, like the forest.

It was a great-great-grand-daughter who read in her grandmother's diary of the family homestead on the banks of the Willamette River. The old clapboard house was gone, she discovered, but beside the porch of the newer brick home grew a bush with small, gray-green leaves and branches weighted down by roses, striped like peppermint candy.

She planted a cutting from the rose in her own garden, and it bloomed two summers later. A friend told her the rose's name.

The next summer she was out in the garden cutting a bouquet when the baby inside stirred, kicked, and seemed to stretch.

The mother smiled and laid her hands across her stomach. She had been unable to think of a name for her daughter, but now she knew.

his daughter would be Rosamund, a part of those who had come before, just as the rose was—a namesake and a memory.

"Rosamund, for the rose," she said, "That's what we'll call you. Rosamund."